OCT   2010

P9-CPW-909

Latin American Celebrations and Festivals

Hispanic Heritage Month
Mes de la Herencia Hispana

Kerrie Logan Hollihan

**Traducción al español:
Ma. Pilar Sanz**

PowerKiDS press. & **Editorial Buenas Letras**™
New York

Published in 2010 by The Rosen Publishing Group, Inc.
29 East 21st Street, New York, NY 10010

First Edition

Editor: Nicole Pristash
Book Design: Greg Tucker
Photo Researcher: Jessica Gerweck

Photo Credits: Cover © Jeff Greenberg/agefotostock; p. 5 © Paddy Eckersley/age fotostock; p. 7 Omar Torres/AFP/Getty Images; p. 9 © Holly Harris/Getty Images; p. 11 Jeff Cadge/Getty Images; p. 13 (main) Alex Wong/Getty Images; p. 13 (inset) Bob Riha Jr./WireImage/Getty Images; p. 15 (main) Scott Boehm/Getty Images; p. 15 (inset) Jon Kopaloff/FilmMagic/Getty Images; p. 17 Marco Secchi/Getty Images; p. 19 Pierre-Philippe Marcou/AFP/Getty Images; p. 21 Juan Silva/Getty Images.

Library of Congress Cataloging-in-Publication Data

Hollihan, Kerrie Logan.
  Hispanic Heritage Month = Mes de la Herencia Hispana / Kerrie Logan Hollihan; traducción al español, Ma. Pilar Sanz. — 1st ed.
    p. cm. — (Latin American celebrations and festivals = Celebraciones y festivales de Latinoamérica)
  Includes index.
  ISBN 978-1-4358-9364-1 (library binding)
  1. Hispanic Heritage Month—Juvenile literature. 2. Hispanic Americans—Juvenile literature. I. Title.
II. Title: Mes de la Herencia Hispana.
  E184.S75H67 2010
  973'.0468—dc22
                              2009030401

Manufactured in the United States of America

CPSIA Compliance Information: Batch #WW10PK: For Further Information contact Rosen Publishing, New York, New York at 1-800-237-9932

CONTENTS

CONTENIDO

During Hispanic **Heritage** Month, many Americans with Hispanic roots **celebrate** their **traditions** and honor their culture. Culture is the way people live. Hispanic Heritage Month is a time for all Americans to celebrate what Hispanics have given to America.

Muchas personas con raíces hispanas, que viven en los Estados Unidos, **celebran** sus **tradiciones** y su cultura durante el Mes de la **Herencia** Hispana. La cultura es la forma en la que viven las personas. El Mes de la Herencia Hispana es el tiempo de celebrar lo que los hispanos le han dado a los Estados Unidos.

Hispanic Heritage Month is a time for Hispanic families to celebrate their culture.

El Mes de la Herencia Hispana es el tiempo para que las familias hispanas celebren su cultura.

During September, several countries in Latin America celebrate their **independence** from Spain. Some of these nations are Costa Rica, El Salvador, Guatemala, Honduras, Nicaragua, Mexico, and Chile. In 1988, the U.S. government named September 15 to October 15 Hispanic Heritage Month.

Muchos países de Latinoamérica celebran su **independencia** de España en el mes de septiembre. Algunos de estos países son Costa Rica, El Salvador, Guatemala, Honduras, Nicaragua, México y Chile. En 1988, el gobierno de los Estados Unidos nombró el Mes de la Herencia Hispana, del 15 de septiembre al 15 de Octubre.

Each September, people gather in Mexico City to celebrate Mexico's independence.

En septiembre, los mexicanos se reúnen en la Ciudad de México para celebrar su independencia.

7

Hispanics, also called Latinos, live in the United States for different reasons. Many Hispanics live in places that were once part of Mexico. Others came from Central America, South America, Mexico, and the Caribbean because they wanted better lives. Other Latinos came to find freedom in America.

Los hispanos, o latinos, viven en los Estados Unidos por muchas razones. Muchos hispanos viven en lugares que fueron parte de México. Otros han llegado de Centroamérica, Sudamérica, México y el Caribe con la idea de mejorar sus vidas. Otros, han llegado en busca de libertad.

Many Hispanics come to America for better jobs or better schools for their children.
Muchos hispanos llegaron a los Estados Unidos buscando mejores escuelas para sus hijos.

Today, about one in eight Americans is Hispanic. Most Hispanics live in the Southwest and in large cities in the Midwest and the Northeast. Like other Americans, Hispanics have many types of jobs. They are doctors, cleaners, salespeople, and reporters.

Actualmente, uno de cada ocho estadounidenses es hispano. La mayoría de los hispanos viven en el sudoeste del país o en grandes ciudades en el oeste o noreste. Al igual que otros estadounidenses, los hispanos tienen muchos tipos de trabajos, como médicos, encargados de limpieza, vendedores o reporteros.

Hispanics hold many different types of jobs in America. This woman is a teacher.

Los hispanos tienen muchos trabajos distintos. Esta mujer es maestra de escuela.

Hispanics have done great things for America. From the 1950s to the 1980s, a Mexican American named César Chávez helped gain rights, such as fair pay and safe places to work, for farm workers. Sonia Sotomayor is the first Hispanic U.S. **Supreme Court** justice.

Los hispanos han hecho grandes cosas en los Estados Unidos. De los años 1950 a 1980, el méxicoamericano César Chávez ayudó a que se respetaran los derechos de los empleados del campo, que recibieran mejor pago y condiciones de trabajo. Sonia Sotomayor es la primera jueza hispana en la **Corte Suprema** de los Estados Unidos.

Sonia Sotomayor's family is Puerto Rican. *Inset*: César Chávez speaks to a crowd.

La familia de Sonia Sotomayor es de Puerto Rico. Recuadro: César Chávez en un discurso.

Many sports players and actors are Hispanic. Tony Romo is a quarterback for the Dallas Cowboys. He is one of the first Hispanics to lead an NFL football team. Selena Gómez, a Hispanic actress, is the star of the Disney Channel show *Wizards of Waverly Place*.

Muchos deportistas y artistas famosos son hispanos. Tony Romo es el mariscal de campo de los Vaqueros de Dallas. Romo es uno de los primeros hispanos en encabezar un equipo de la NFL. Selena Gómez es actriz. Gómez es la estrella del programa de televisión *Wizards of Waverly Place* en el canal Disney.

Tony Romo's father is Mexican. *Inset*: Selena Gómez is a young Mexican-American star.

El papá de Tony Romo es mexicano. Recuadro, Selena Gómez es méxicoamericana.

Hispanic culture has had an impact on art, music, and dance in America. Hispanic artists paint, draw, and take pictures. Salsa, a popular type of dance and music in the United States, has roots in the Caribbean. The tango, another type of popular dance, came out of Argentina.

La cultura hispana ha influenciado todas las disciplinas artísticas de los Estados Unidos. Los artistas hispanos pintan, dibujan y toman fotografías. La música salsa, que tiene sus raíces en el caribe, es muy popular en los Estados Unidos. El tango, otro tipo de baile muy popular, es originario de Argentina.

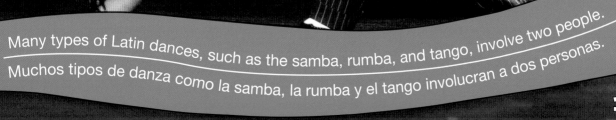

Many types of Latin dances, such as the samba, rumba, and tango, involve two people.

Muchos tipos de danza como la samba, la rumba y el tango involucran a dos personas.

One of the most important days of Hispanic Heritage Month is *Día de la Raza* (DEE-ah DAY LAH RAH-sah), or Day of the Race, on October 12. This day marks Christopher Columbus's arrival in the Americas. Many Hispanics use this day to reconnect with their heritage.

Uno de los días más importantes del Mes de la Herencia Hispana es el Día de la Raza, el 12 de octubre. En este día se celebra la llegada de Cristóbal Colón al continente americano. Muchos hispanos usan el Día de la Raza para reconectarse con sus raices.

These dancers from Bolivia are taking part in a parade to celebrate Día de la Raza.

Estos bailarines de Bolivia participan en un festival en el que se celebra el Día de la Raza.

There are many things that you can do to learn more about Hispanic culture during Hispanic Heritage Month and all year long. You can visit a museum and see Hispanic art, listen to Latin music, learn a Latin dance, or watch a movie in Spanish.

Hay muchas cosas que puedes aprender sobre la cultura hispana durante el Mes de la Herencia Hispana, y en el resto del año. Puedes visitar museos de arte hispano, escuchar música, aprender un baile de Latinoamérica, o hasta ver una película en español.

Visiting a museum, as this boy is doing, can teach you about Hispanic culture.

Visitar un museo, como lo hace este chico, ayuda a aprender sobre la cultura hispana.

Americans whose families came from Latin America have a strong heritage. Hispanics' contributions are an important part of U.S. history. Their culture add richness to American life. Hispanic Heritage Month offers all Americans a chance to celebrate them.

Los estadounidenses cuyas familias vienen de Latinoamérica tienen una herencia cultural muy fuerte. La contribución de los hispanos es una parte muy importante de la historia de los Estados Unidos. La cultura hispana enriquecen la vida en los Estados Unidos. El Mes de la Herencia Hispana es una gran oportunidad para celebrarlo.

Glossary

celebrate (SEH-leh-brayt) To honor an important moment by doing special things.

heritage (HER-uh-tij) The cultural traditions passed from parent to child.

independence (in-dih-PEN-dents) Freedom from the control or support of other people.

Supreme Court (suh-PREEM KORT) The highest court in the United States.

traditions (truh-DIH-shunz) Ways of doing things that have been passed down over time.

Glosario

celebrar Hacer algo especial para reconocer un momento importante.

Corte Suprema (la) La corte de mayor autoridad en los Estados Unidos.

herencia (la) Las tradiciones culturales pasadas de padres a hijos.

independencia (la) Libertad del control o apoyo de otra persona, grupo o país.

tradiciones (las) Manera de hacer las cosas que ha sido transmitida a través del paso del tiempo.

Index

Índice

Web Sites /
Páginas de Internet

Due to the changing nature of Internet links, PowerKids Press has developed an online list of Web sites related to the subject of this book. This site is updated regularly. Please use this link to access the list:
www.powerkidslinks.com/lacf/heritage/